How the West Was Black

ISBN: 978-1-956076-06-6

PROOFREADING and CREATIVE DIRECTION by NaBeela Washington
PROOFREADING by Faith Brown
COVER ART by Alania Hinckson
ISSUE DESIGN and LAYOUT by Samantha Hambleton
GUEST EDITING by Morgan Christie

A Black writer and art collector, NaBeela Washington holds a Master's in Creative Writing and English from Southern New Hampshire University and a Bachelor's in Visual Advertising from The University of Alabama at Birmingham. She is the Founder of *Lucky Jefferson*.

Alania Caridad Hinckson is a visual artist from Jackson Heights, NYC. She attends MICA and studies Illustration and Sequential Arts.

Morgan Christie is the author of "Boolean Logic", the Howling Bird Press Nonfiction Prize winner, "These Bodies" (Tolsun Books, 2020), a Hurston Wright Legacy Award nominee, and four poetry chapbooks. She was awarded the 2022 Arc Poem of the Year prize and Digging Press's Chapbook Series Prize.

Samantha Hambleton is a recent graduate from the University of St Andrews in Scotland. She is now based in Detroit and is looking forward to entering the literary world. Passionate about all things sustainability and social justice, Samantha is honored to have the opportunity to support Lucky Jefferson's mission.

Faith Brown is a poet & editor from NYC. She holds an MFA from City College where she was awarded The Jerome Lowell DeJur Prize for her poetry manuscript. She is also on twitter @_faithestella.

Publication of *Lucky Jefferson* is made possible through community support.

Donate or submit to *Lucky Jefferson* on our website: luckyjefferson.com.

Foreword

Exploring new narratives of the West through the lens of Blackness, *How the West Was Black* is not just a reimagining of historical landscapes —it's a reclamation of stories untold and voices unheard. It underscores the vital role of reshaping our understanding of history and culture. By casting Black bounty hunters as the heroes of the New Frontier, this series challenges the traditional narratives and invites us to envision a world where justice reigns. This is more than important—it's essential—as it opens up a space for new stories to flourish, ensuring that our collective history is rewritten through the truth; with the perspectives of those who have long been buried beneath marginalization.

How the West Was Black, Issue 5 of *Awake*, illustrates the transformative power of Blackness in shaping the history of the West, and our future. Our nine bounty hunters take us on journeys to places beyond the typical imagination, expanding the genre's horizons.

This issue pushes past traditional boundaries of storytelling, introducing you to a world where there are no limits to how far or where your imagination can take you.

If you've enjoyed modern westerns like Greg Neri's adaptation of *Concrete Cowboy*, cross-genre works like Jordan Peele's *Nope*, or even traditional/ revisionist westerns such as Jeymes Samuel's *The Harder They Fall*, then this issue is for you.

The works within transport readers to a reality where Black bounty hunters can finally conquer 'isms' that have oppressed our world, once and for all.

NaBeela Washington
Editor-in-Chief

bounty hunters

We Joog
Chris L. Butler

inside the walls of this crunchy saloon / lie saturday night hearts filled with angst /Folks/ frustrated from the inflation / even the rule / makers are filled with hatred / inside the walls of this raggedy tavern are sons and daughters / whose families didn't pay enough attention like a dog fighting for a glance from their owner's / fixated brow ogling some stupid app on their iphone / inside the walls of this decrepit dive bar / are pirates / with peg legs / looking—to feast on someone's trauma / in the name of personal satisfaction / yes, this is a tavern that matches the reality of our society / there is nothing / perfect inside of it / except / for the highest proof libation / dangling out of the bottle into your cup like a Vince Carter Dunk / liquor waterfall rush of 99 bananas, or everclear / or some other shit that probably would be better suited to disinfect blacktop scrapes or war wounds / this bar gives / about as many fucks as this prose stream of consciousness is attempting to care less about overwhelming your senses / with this appetizer platter's worth of images / to explain the decrepitness of this retro fitted arcade where you can blaze / where every Saturday a group of bridesmaids are in here getting white girl wasted / on Mike's Hard Lemonade while *Lemonade* by Beyoncé plays over the loudspeakers / even though these days we are in the *Renaissance* age / nonetheless / hits are hits / we joog and jive / and vibe as her lyrics ooze out of the pores inside the DJ's speakers / we tune out the feedback it gives off / because we know this is a jank ass hookah lounge / the spot in which we fell in love / and when this mutha shut down / we rode / down the backway of Alabama Street in that Lyft / the driver was turnt when he heard us say we were going to eat at the Houston Breakfast Klub. the squad wasn't into all of that and Braxton is allergic to half of everything on the menu so when the Lyft driver dropped us off / we decided to dip like that Freak Nasty song / which was coincidentally / played earlier in that hookah bar that we were just at a place where the smoke was thicker than chocolate tapioca pudding / but regret, was not /

Still Not Beautiful

Kei Vough Korede

We wake in cultivated silence,
blue morality conditioned by liquors.
We know Grief is the mother
of hangovers—an interloper of glee.
My head throbs, a stampede of demons
pounding inside; aching with the labor of existing.
We use painkillers even though
they won't still the pain of living.
Often, I plod into my deplorable past:
How I lived a closeted life in terror of being
a casualty of familial condescension.
Having pardoned my miseducation,
you curtail my excesses to be with me,
replace my grief with gay,
my caprice with equanimity,
hence compelling my joy into existence.
What insistence glory you harbour,
lover? That theatrics through
which you propel me into quotidian excellence.

Five and None

Jacob Mack

The last rays of glittering sunlight were slowly slipping from the town, like sand through fingertips. About a quarter mile from the train station, the Waylon house sat chipped and raw from years of weathering. In the attic, Marlon rested the rifle just below the only window. The revolver stayed tucked into his waistband.

He looked out the window, facing the only road to the house. He knew, he hoped, that he would be able to hear them coming, but a vigilant eye wouldn't hurt. Might prove the difference. He put his hands on the window sill and felt the old wood creak from the pressure.

He turned from the window as the attic's trap door popped open. His hand instinctively went to his back, rested when he saw Henry's face pop out.

"Just me," Henry said, eyeing him warily. Once he had climbed in, he reached back down into the opening and produced a plate with a few slices of bread and an orange. "Brought you some food, like I said." He held it out to Marlon, who grabbed it with one hand. Marlon stayed standing, holding the plate with one hand and grabbing a piece of bread off of it with the other.

"Ain't much," Henry added, and shrugged. He stayed on the ground, hands resting on his knees.

"Thank you," Marlon finally muttered through a mouthful. Henry nodded.

The two men sat in silence while Marlon ate. His eyes only went from the plate, the food, to the window. Mechanically, he took a look out after every bite. He peeled the orange by cutting into them with his thumb, taking care not to squeeze out the juice. He put the peel back onto the plate. When he finished, he handed the plate back to Henry, who took it and set it on the attic floor beside himself.

"So," Henry began, rubbing the back of his neck.

"When am I leaving?" Marlon said, looking out the window. It was a question, but he spoke it like an answer.

"Yeah," Henry said, and stopped rubbing. He stared at the back of Marlon's head as the latter rested his arms on the sill. Henry's eyes shifted down to the rifle quickly before looking back up.

"When they get here," Marlon responded.

"It'll be plum late by then, won't it?"

Marlon didn't answer but continued keeping watch. A stray piece of the breeze caught the window sill and came into the attic, and Henry shuddered.

"How many bullets you got left?" He asked.

"Five in the rifle, none in the revolver."

Six from the revolver, from the inciting incident and then the escape. Cutting through an alley on his way to work, the Mckinley brothers tried to put a bag over his head. It took one shot for the first brother, right to the head, but the other took two, both in the chest.

His actions were instinctual; the people in town said animalistic, but there's nothing animal about a gun.

Then he'd used the last bullets covering his way out of town. He was smart enough to not waste any, especially when he was already in such want. Men had come running right after the first shot, but to most of them he was little more than kicked-up dust. Old Sam Peters, who had been gunning for the sheriff position too hard to ever get it, was the only one who could keep up with him. For him, Marlon had taken two shots, both of which missed. The first bought him enough time to get back to his horse, and the second would've caught Old Sam right between the eyes, if he hadn't caught the glint of the metal just quick enough to duck.

Three from the rifle, during his first last stand in the valley. He fired one warning shot at the five men, Old Sam among 'em, that had come for him. Then one of them got it in the leg, and another in the chest, on the other side of his heart. That had spooked them into leaving with the wounded and getting the sheriff. He then made his way to Henry's house, where he knew they'd eventually find him again.

He'd kept any extra ammunition in the cabin, which he knew was probably cinders by then.

"I'd offer you some more, but you know I don't got nothing," Henry said, talking either about the food or the guns. Marlon only nodded.

"You know I'm a friend, Marlon," Henry said, "And I don't mind having you. But maybe you need to-" he started, then stopped. "It would be better for everyone, you and me."

"Too late," Marlon responded, still looking out. "They're here." He saw a speck on the horizon, moving fast.

"Damn it all to hell!" Henry shouted, and jumped up. Though Marlon didn't look at him, his face had turned to a pale red.

"You causing me and mine too much trouble, Marlon." Venom seeped into his voice. "I ain't goin' down for no damn n—er."

Henry pulled a small knife from his pocket and lunged at Marlon's right side. He brought the blade down in an arcing motion, but found his wrist stopped with almost enough force to snap it. Henry felt a searing in his stomach, and stumbled backwards. He fell to the ground, landing almost in the same spot he had first sat. The sizzle of the gunpowder cut through the silence as Marlon looked down at him.

"Five and one," he mumbled to himself. "Five and one."

He set the revolver down and picked up the rifle. They were more than just a speck now, and he could make out that there were about ten of them: the three that had escaped unharmed last time, the sheriff, a couple deputies, and a few new faces besides. Right beside the sheriff, leading the charge, was Old Sam. Marlon lined up a shot and held his breath.

Who Shot Ya?

A. Brown

There were two photos of Pac being circulated on bounty posters. In both, he held a pistol close to his face and a bandana tied around his head, just beneath his hat. Pac smoked freshly rolled tobacco and counted a fistful of money. He was little more than an imaginary friend, something that filled in Wynn's empty spaces just like he filled in everyone else's. Nellie missed seeing posters where his eyes were at their largest, swollen with curiosity and full of wisdom, of life. And the ones where he smiled like he was meeting The Mother herself had long faded into obscurity. The only remaining copies hung above Wynn's bed. The same one she'd died in.

"I won't deny it, I'm a straight ridah, you don't wanna fuck with me." Nellie could hear Wynn's voice all around her. There were other lyrics to that old song, but those were Wynn's favorite. Especially the "you don't wanna fuck with me." Wynn chewed that one up and spit it out like dip. Nellie imagined it was Wynn's war cry when she and her gang went out and fucked shit up, though she just saw it as handling business. The words lingered in the air around them like dust.

By the time Wynn birthed Nellie, those days were in the past. Nellie had only heard stories about that side of her mother, whispered from the mouths of strangers in their tiny settlement. Stories of Wynn's hands soaked in blood: how she'd sent a single bullet through the throats of three men, how she'd rode at the front of a gang of women, twenty-five deep, brave enough to ride through any town with their faces uncovered since they'd likely just rob it blind.

Nellie only knew Wynn as the woman who sat her down and brushed her hair smooth once a week; who worked on a small ranch swathing oats and separating them from the stem; who pulled blue oaks from the ground with her bare hands, chopped them into lumber and firewood, and carried any extra to the elderly couple a mile up the road. Wynn taught Nellie to shoot, often in the dead of night—made her pay attention to what she heard more than what she saw. Wynn was the person who cradled Nellie in arms toned by labor, made her feel both strong and delicate. The woman who hosted monthly card games where Nellie watched her mother's friend group dwindle from the crack in her bedroom door jamb. One by one, Wynn's friends stopped dropping by for spiced apples and Spades. Started turning up floating face down in rivers, or with their limbs tangled high in trees. Shot. Drowned.

They came for Wynn just after Nellie's twentieth birthday. While Nellie was out, they dragged Wynn to the basement of an abandoned saloon, beat her purple and left her to die. When Nellie found her, her voice was a whisper, her breath merely a breeze. Nellie loaded her into a shallow wagon and took her home. Laid her in the bed, Pac's eyes wide and watching from her favorite poster—one Wynn found being distributed in a town with nothing else to offer..

Wynn had prepared Nellie for this moment. She grabbed the locket from her mother's bedside table and gently pulled Wynn's spirit from her lips like fingertips coaxing out a splinter. Her spirit—strong, black, with tinges of red and blue—fit perfectly into the space in the locket. Nellie wondered what it would have looked like if she'd seen it before Wynn turned things around. If there would have been more red, more blue. Less black. Nellie paused as she shut the door to her mother's bedroom and listened carefully, eyes scanning the darkness. Her ears twitched as she heard a slow, high-pitched whistle from within the house: a tune she remembered from her mother's sleepless nights, when she paced the front room mumbling, "Saw me in the drop, three and a quarter. Slaughter, electrical tape around your daughter."

Nellie moved quickly, pulled the pistol from her holster, and fired five quick shots, leaving a single bullet in the cylinder, just in case she'd missed. The intruder collapsed to the ground, his pistol sliding across the floor. She wrestled a set of matches from her pocket and lit the lantern hanging on the sitting room wall.

The man writhed on the floor, his hands shook as they pressed against the gunshot wound on his side. Nellie figured she had until sunrise before the rest of his crew rose from the dirt, pistols in hand and rained down on the house like a storm. She kept the gun on him until his chest stopped rising and his hands were flat against his stomach, his screaming ceased. Until he had given her a life for the one he'd stolen.

When morning came, Nellie climbed onto her horse, gathering the reigns into her hands. Tucked between the skin of her hips and the waist of her jeans, Pac's smile sat, folded into the seam of a bounty poster. A photo of her mother sat comfortably behind it. In it, Wynn's—hair was in a single braid dangled over her shoulder, a bundle of firewood hugged against her chest like her only daughter. And she smiled. Nellie wondered if this was the photo they had used on her bounty posters, or if they dug up one that Nellie had never seen, one where Wynn carried a shotgun on her shoulders and bared her teeth. Where she beat someone's head with a brick or smoked a rolled cigarette over a fresh corpse.

"I won't deny it, I'm a straight ridah," Nellie mumbled, her eyes settling on where the horizon spat out the sun. Her voice wasn't as rich as Wynn's had been, it didn't hold that same power. Still, Nellie held onto the locket around her neck and sat up higher on her horse. Said, "You don't wanna fuck with me."

Elsie

Dana Tenille Weekes

you should be a bagger when you grow up

man tells child
momma says to cashier *stop*

momma turns from cashier to bagger
momma asks man to repeat

child watches momma
child turns from momma to man

man repeats
black momma intercoms the ancestors

white man should pray

Speechless
Jaimie Wilson

Coming home from Carlisle School
to Rosebud Reservation, a big boy
after five years of haircuts, prayer, and standing in line.
I will find a job, be useful now.
I step off the train into Grandmother's arms,
smelling wood smoke, frybread grease,
feeling my short hair clutched between her rough fingers.
Hoksila wan ktepi, she mutters.
What did she say?
I have forgotten the words.
That wind has ceased to blow in me.

Someone Planted An Idea About Me

(line from **The Tradition** by Jericho Brown)

Regina Jamison

and I bucked against the shaping of it
rolled up my sleeves, removed my earrings
when the white teacher called us animals

                I watched *Roots* & dug holes
                some seeds planted, not gonna let them
                germinate propagate contaminate

dirt under nails and foot
I watch them watch me, better watch out
cuz I'm comin'

Reverse Racism

Linda Trice

Brutus stood in the opening of a cave.

His son, Sonny, a brawny married man of twenty three was back home, gathering information. So was his wife Jenny. They wanted to know who was going West, when they were leaving, who they were selling their store and land to.

Jenny took in laundry but not many folks in Danville used her services now. Some wanted her services without paying her. They'd been her best customers back when things were better.

Jenny nodded. Yes, they had been good customers, and she'd been a good laundress but things were different now.

The white women argued and Jenny just looked at them, saying nothing. They turned away, some mumbling cruel words as they left.

The owner of the dry goods store left with his family. No one would buy his shop so he and his family just abandoned it. They were going West. They were going where gold could be picked out of a stream. That's what the newspapers said.

That's what Old Man Jacob said. He'd been there. Out West. The place where gold glimmered in creeks. Food grew out of the earth almost as soon as you planted the seeds. That's what Old Man Jacob said.

The farmers believed him. "A place where food was abundant. Grew out of the early as soon as you planted the seeds". They repeated what the old man said. He'd been there. He had to know. Why some said that Old Man Jacob said he'd actually seen corn grow up towards the sky, right before his eyes. And Old Man Jacob never lied.

"If Out West is so grand why'd Jacob come back?" Spinster Sarah grumbled as she stood on the steps of Rising Sun Baptist Church after services one Sunday.

"Oh, don't listen to her," Mandy told the other women. "She's mad because Jacob didn't marry her."

The other women giggled in their handkerchiefs then continued down the stairs. They had things to do—food to can, baskets to pack. They were leaving in the morning. "Out West" people heard Mandy murmur.

II

Danville was quiet. The white folks had gone. Those that could sell their land, their shops, did so. Most got far less than they thought they should have gotten. But they were in a hurry. Out West was waiting,
Brutus came back to Danville one night. He'd seen the white folks of Danville in their covered wagons leading a cow for the baby's milk and sometimes a few chickens just in case

III

Pistol Will and his men got Mandy's wagon one night. Brutus had given them the right information. Mandy's folk were easy pickens.
They left her with her kin, sitting on the ground near a cactus. They took the wagon, cow and chickens. Cookie made a banquet for them that night. He was the one who told them about Brutus.
Two nights later Farmer Ed and his kin found themselves sitting on the ground, Cookie made corn pone as the special dish that night. He knew how much Pistol Will liked his corn pone.

IV

Brutus came back to Danville. His family settled into Farmer Ed's farm. His nephew ran the dry goods shop. His nieces made biscuits, pies and all sorts of good things to eat.
Prospectors came to Danville. They'd heard that that the folks were kind. After all, they'd all been enslaved or married folks who had been.
The white folks of Danville never returned. The Black folks renamed their town, OURS.

a modern haiku

Adele Nwankwo

stepping / into / new / pronouns / wild / grass

INTERIOR ARTWORK by Ro Hegarty, Kristine Pham, and KK Farinola

Royce Hegarty is a digital illustrator who explores genres of fantasy, sci-fi and horror with a candy-colored palette, high contrast, and tight linework.

Kristine "Kris" Pham is an illustrator and 2D animator in the greater Philadelphia region. She completed her BFA in Illustration and Minor in Animation at the University of the Arts. Her work has been described as a bold personality contained by calm lines.

KK is an American Illustrator & Designer based in New England.

Write down your favorite title from a piece
on pages 13-37. Use this title to write a new poem
(or story) that isn't about the subject
matter of the original piece

SUBMIT TO LUCKY JEFFERSON

Lucky Jefferson's mission is simple:
we publish social change.

And our vision is to see books reimagined to
center the modern reader.

Founded in 2018, *Lucky Jefferson* is an award-winning
nonprofit, literary journal, and publisher that reimagines
books by creating interactive and collaborative community
experiences that center the writer and artist and cultivate
inclusion and representation in contemporary literature.

Lucky Jefferson is proud to feature poets and writers who
have never been published, marginalized perspectives, and
those who sought to pursue writing later in life.

Learn more + consider submitting at: **luckyjefferson.com**

FOLLOW US

 @lucky_jefferson

 @_luckyjefferson

 @luckyjeffersonlit

STRIKE A POSE

take a selfie
with your copy of
How the West was Black
and tag us!

HASHTAGSSSS

use #AWAKE5,
#HowTheWestWasBlack,
or #LJSQUAD to
follow the convo

www.ingramcontent.com/pod-product-compliance
Lightning Source LLC
Chambersburg PA
CBHW071352200726
48293CB00008B/2615